Reap What You Sow

A play for children

12 YEARS +

By George Njimele

"… a readable piece of work," Dr Yosimbom Hassan

"… a masterpiece," Nformi Nganjo

Peacock Writers Series
P.O. Box 3092 Bonaberi, Douala, Cameroon
Tel: (237) 67752 72 36
Email: georgenjimele@gmail.com

First published 2022

© Peacock Writers Series

ISBN: 978-9956-540-16-7

Cover design by Theo Mark

About the author

Njimele was born in Awing, North West Region Cameroon in 1973. He started writing at an early age, and he writes mostly for children and young adults. He took up writing full-time and started the Peacock Writers Series in Cameroon. He won the National Prize for poetry in 1995 organized by the National Book Development Council. Some of his works viz, *Madmen and Traitors* (2015), *The Queen of Power* (1998), *Undeserved Suffering* (2008), *The Slave Boys* (2008) and *Poverty is Crazy* (2012) are prescribed in the Cameroon school curriculum (literature awareness) for beginners in secondary school. His other works include: *King Shaba* (2006), *House of Peace* (2007), *Land of Sweet Meat* (2017), *A Time to Reconcile* (2020), *Reap What You Sow* (2020). His other works, *The Lion and the Tortoise and Other Stories* and *Nyamsi and His Grandson* were selected for the Cameroon/World Bank Read-at-Home Project in 2021. He lives with his family in Douala, Cameroon.

An overview by
Dr Eleanor Dasi Yaoundé University I

In these modern times, when African children are increasingly being exposed to western lifestyles, African parents are faced with the dilemma of letting the children have their way or raising them in the strict demands of African traditional values. Njimele's *Reap What You Sow* revolves around the difficulties a mother faces raising children according to traditional African standards, particularly when the father seems to flow along with the relaxation of the rules.

To teenagers, the play warns against keeping bad friends, engaging early in sexual activity, drinking alcohol, as these would only bring disaster to those who indulge in them – crime, unwanted pregnancies, etc. Micara and Dinga both get pregnant at early ages, which certainly disrupts their education and plays on their future, while Pesou gets entangled in a story of burglary and Sala risks prison for robbery and getting the two girls pregnant at the same time.

The play leaves readers asking what has become of the morality that accompanies the raising of children in a traditional African context; how can we redefine the African personhood corrupted by modernity? How do we cope with the fiercely independent breed of children these days; their alignment with globalising forces and their addiction to modern gadgets?

It is true that we are in an era in which the effects of modernity are enormous on African children which oftentimes block them from understanding boundaries and limitations. This should not however stop them from listening to their parents particularly,

iv

their mothers, who in most African cultures, are the primary child raisers. That is why when the play opens, Mrs Batou is worried about the conduct of her children.

Children in their early teens will read and understand the necessity of obeying their mothers' instructions because as primary care-givers, added to the maternal bond, mothers are mostly loving and devoted and so always want the best for their children - guiding them in the right direction. The children on their part, will also learn to form a healthy relationship with their parents which will enable both parties to be confident in their dealings with the other. Pesou, for example, understands that it is unlawful for his father to claim ownership of a rifle that he picked up, but he does not attempt to tell him so. The father later gets entangled in a setup that costs him a huge sum of money to bail himself out.

Apart from the struggles of parents in teaching their children fundamental moral values, *Reap What You Sow* also exposes the corruption, conspiracy and other social ills that plague post-independent African societies. A soldier gets drunk and abandons his rifle in a bar; Mr Batou finds and keeps it but is betrayed by Sala; the law enforcement officers are interested in receiving money from Mr Batou to close the case while Mrs Bamen uses her position and influence to destroy case files.

However, in exposing these problems, the author is suggesting that for these to be avoided, children must learn to properly socialise, behave well, communicate politely and confidently, be disciplined and to engage in activities that will take them away from the addiction to modern gadgets. This way, they will build a community that will not be prone to crime and delinquency.

Table of Contents

Characters vii

Act One, Scene 1 1

Scene 2 7

Scene 3 12

Act Two, Scene 1 20

Scene 2 28

Scene 3 34

Act Three, Scene 1 39

Scene 2 43

Scene 3 49

Scene 4 51

Scene 5 55

Characters

Mr Batou	– a middle-aged state agent
Mrs Batou	– his wife
Micara	– first daughter to the Batous
Pata	– second daughter to the Batous
Pesou	– a son to the Batous
Mrs Bamen	– Mrs Batou's friend
Dinga	– Mrs Bamen's daughter
Mbola	– Mr Batou's elder brother
Sala	– a wayward young man
Policemen	– Constable Pokem
	– Inspector Wokem

ACT ONE

Scene 1

A rectangular and ostentatious sitting room comes into view. At its centre are fabric sofas and a polyester carpet. Other noticeable objects include: a wall clock, a calendar, a lady's portrait and family pictures. The setting should portray a house with an admirable outlook. Mr Batou is at home, lying low. He sits on one of the sofas, scrolling a text on his smart phone. Mrs Batou emerges, wearing a light-weight house dress, a velvet headscarf, and sheepskin slippers.

Mrs Batou:	(*Frowning.*) My husband, my heart is heavy with a big worry.
Mr Batou:	(*Astonished.*) Ah! What's your worry about, my dear?
Mrs Batou:	The conduct of our children has fallen short of expectations.
Mr Batou:	(*Tilts his head forward.*) Tell me, you certainly have some bad news!
Mrs Batou:	Not bad news really, but a lot of crooked things that we must put straight.
Mr Batou:	Crooked things? Okay, I'm all ears.
Mrs Batou:	It's no news to you that our marriage has been blessed with three children - two girls and a boy, to be exact.
Mr Batou:	That's right!
Mrs Batou:	After the birth of our lastborn, you and I decided to stop further delivery for fear of me losing my life on a midwife's table.

1

Mr Batou:	Perfectly correct, my dear wife! It was a timely decision, reached after much re-flection. The aim was to avoid a caesarian delivery which is no more a life-saving option.
Mrs Batou:	Excellent! Despite such a consideration, you know I still love to make more children, don't you?
Mr Batou:	I know, and I would rejoice like the birds in the sky if we make five more kids. In fact, I would be happier than any Olympic gold medalist.
Mrs Batou:	My mum was a lucky maker of children. She birthed nine children, none through caesarian delivery.
Mr Batou:	That's true, my dear wife, but you can't compare past happenings with what prevails now. That was their time (a time when human life mattered most). Your mum lived essentially on natural food, you know, don't you?
Mrs Batou:	I do.
Mr Batou:	She never smoked tobacco. And as an expectant mother, she avoided taking in too much alcoholic drinks.
Mrs Batou:	You have pertinent observations, but there are other reasons for these risky deliveries. Believe me, one of such reasons is the hunger for riches. Many doctors want to own flashy cars…Volvo, Lexus, Ferrari, BMW, Audi, Land Rover, etc. They covet costly houses with luxurious amenities.

	They like houses that are built in optimal locations, decorated with high-end equipment.
Mr Batou:	It is their intention to take lives; they want rather the money!
Mrs Batou:	It's a pity, my husband! I'm obliged to live with three children, against my own will. Yes, only three children, none of whom is all right in terms of good morals, good sense, sound understanding and wisdom.
Mr Batou:	(*Disturbed.*) My goodness! I don't like the way you sound. Good morals, good sense, sound understanding and wisdom! Is it possible for a single individual to have all these attributes? Even you, seated by me, do you have a good dose of good morals, good sense, sound understanding and wisdom?
Mrs Batou:	Why not? Except you want to belittle my worth. Experience and age have given me enough good sense, understanding and wisdom.
Mr Batou:	Aha, I am glad you talk about age and experience. Are our children experienced and mature in age? Does an egg hatch into a chick without incubation? You know the times in which we live. These are times of distraction and disorder with the youth.
Mrs Batou:	You believe good sense and understanding come with age. I disagree! My friend, Mrs Bamen, has reasonable and well-behaved

children. Dinga is a beautiful and clever girl. She doesn't mess around like her friend, Micara. She doesn't wriggle her bottom to seduce boys.

Mr Batou:	Ah! Have you lived with her? You know what still waters can do. She might be a disguised imposter. All children are gifts from Heaven. Heaven alone can determine the content of their hearts and their minds. Comparing them is questioning the creative ingenuity of the gods. The hen that emulates the swimming skills of a duck will drown in the sea.
Mrs Batou:	We use the gods to justify matters prompted by our own actions. Let's leave the gods alone! They too deserve rest and calm. They have their own troubles to resolve.
Mr Batou:	My dear wife, the gods are our guardians! They cover us against harm. They can't overlook our deeds.
Mrs Batou:	There's an external hand in the actions of these children. I suspect a curse in this home. There's no doubt about it.
Mr Batou:	A curse! Then we're saying the same thing. Curses come from the gods.
Mrs Batou:	But who bears these curses? Every bad fate has an origin. I believe one of us is carrying a curse. And that's what is destroying our children. And in all sincerity, I have no hand in this bad fate.
Mr Batou:	(*Retorting.*) Oh, woman, you're insinuating

	that I'm a curse bearer!
Mrs Batou:	I haven't made any direct accusation against you!
Mr Batou:	OK, let's assume you made an indirect one! So, what's the difference between a direct and an indirect accusation? For me, it's the same like saying I drink beer without naming the type of beer.
Mrs Batou:	You're taking my point too far! I'm simply saying that I have clean hands if this issue involves ancestral curses.
Mr Batou:	What makes you think you don't have a hand in what is happening?
Mrs Batou:	I keep all my actions under control. In other words, I have authority over my emotions and my actins. From early childhood to this day, my thoughts, feelings and deeds are blameless. No blame whatever can be levelled against me.
Mr Batou:	Let me remind you that these children came forth through our marriage. No woman makes a child by herself. No man either. Our marriage was consecrated by the church, and legalised in a competent court. It equally got the approval of the traditional council. And then, it was consummated and blessed with three kids. So, this is not a forged or illicit union. How dare you blame me on the conduct of the children? They bear my genes, and yours as well. Anyway, the lion that devours its own cub never approves of the deed.

5

Mrs Batou:	Ah, by that, you're heaping the blame on me, aren't you?
Mr Batou:	I won't say no, because you've decided to be judge and jury.
Mrs Batou:	You aren't the sole cause of what's happening. Blame it as well on your ancestors!
Mr Batou:	On my own ancestors, and not yours! OK, we'll check and crosscheck our various family histories. With the approach of moonlight, we'll sort out all the wolves killing and eating our sheep.
Mrs Batou:	Be courageous enough to stand the truth!
Mr Batou;	Ha, you keep accusing me? (*He walks out in anger.*)

Scene 2

The setting is as in the previous scene (Mrs Batou's sitting room). Two cheerful girls are standing in the room, ready to enact something. The entire place smells of fragrant perfumes and roll-ons. Pata, the younger girl, wears low-heeled shoes, red socks and a sleeveless, sexy gown. She is slightly built; has a gap in her upper front teeth; has an average height, and an ebony skin. Like her sister, she is markedly beautiful. Both girls have enhanced their beauty with braids, jewels, eye shadows, creams, lotions and manicure. Micara is dressed in a chic, ballet dress, which descends to knee level. They both wear baseball caps with the bills turned backwards. Micara makes towards the wall cupboard, reaches for the CD player and turns it on. A latest hip-hop song starts playing. She turns up the volume. They begin swaying, twerking and singing as the melodies touch their souls. Micara contorts and spins her curves in an enticing manner. Pata lifts and lowers her hands with grace, wriggles her waist. Mrs Batou comes forth unnoticed and is spying on them through the window. She gets enough view of their action and then makes towards the door and presses it open. The girls seem unsatisfied with their fun. Micara hurriedly turns off the CD player.

Mrs Batou: (*She is worried.*) Aha, this is what you're good at! Crazy dancing! You dance like street girls with no manners! This is what my children know best. Poor little me! In fact,

7

	I feel like going insane with your actions. As a mum, I'm proud of nothing, nothing at all! Where can this take you?
Micara:	Ah, you look cute! I like your hairdo.
Mrs Batou:	Leave my hairdo alone! I hate flattery and white lies. Let's talk about this crazy dance you were enacting.
Pata:	Mum, we studied before having fun.
Micara:	Mum, that's true. After studying, we decided to amuse ourselves.
Mrs Batou:	Liars! You always tell lies to escape blame.
Micara:	We're not liars, Mum. I, for one, studied.
Pata:	I revised my history lessons.
Mrs Batou:	Let's assume you studied. Thereafter, why didn't you choose something better for your fun?
Micara:	What do you mean by something better, Mum?
Pata:	(*Smiling.*) I guess she is talking of things she likes… church songs, and maybe, listening to birthday songs and Christmas carols and singing funeral songs.
Micara:	Wow, she is perhaps fond of that! We have our own things we like.
Mrs Batou:	Pata, I haven't assigned you to answer questions on my behalf. So, keep your mouth shut!
Pata:	Ha, Mum, you're different today!

	Mama est vraiment fâchée!
Mrs Batou:	(*She ignores her.*) Why is music your utmost choice for fun?
Pata:	We love music, mostly hit songs from pop, hip-hop, rock, R&B, rhumba, etc.
Mrs Batou:	OK, you mean music with boom, boom sounds? Music with immoral message? Is that what you like? To me, the song you were dancing to isn't a musical piece at all. I heard a clatter of jumbled instruments, aimed at distracting those who lack focus.
Micara:	Ha-ha! No, no, no, Mum. That's high quality music.
Pata:	Mum, we don't dance to bad music! Pop music is what we like, and it's sweet in the ears.
Micara:	That song has won several awards home and abroad.
Mrs Batou:	It can't win anything where I'm part of the jury. Learn to listen to good music, please.
Micara:	OK, what are your preferred musical genres, Mum?
Mrs Batou:	You can listen and dance to Afrobeat, blues, jazz, highlife, rhumba and makossa.
Micara:	Mum, some of the artists playing these genres have boring songs.
Pata:	Songs for elderly people, ha! Songs

Mum is really angry.

9

	for people who like talking about the good old days.
Mrs Batou:	Good music, in addition to melody, must have good message. I some-times listen to your so-called rappers. Some try to criticise the ills of society in their songs. They deserve a pat on the back. Others are caught doing the very things they condemn. And these are people you follow as models!
Micara:	Good music should be danceable. It should have fast rhythms and nice melodies.
Mrs Batou:	Instead of learning how to cook, or doing other useful things, you spend all your time dancing. Can you make a living by dancing? Can dancing foot your bills? Does stepping forward and backward, twisting the waist and swaying the buttocks yield profit?
Pata:	Mum, dancing has become a real profession.
Micara:	I know many well-paid professional dancers.
Mrs Batou:	Even if people make money by dancing, I can't recommend it as a job for any of you. I see it as a crafty strategy for prostitution.
Pata:	(*She turns and complains in an aside.*) She'll never change! Always criticising and doubting! It's hell to

live beside this kind of person. She isn't ready to abandon her queer and old ways.

Mrs Batou: You, Micara, I'm not happy with you! As the elder, aren't you ashamed of yourself? You like messing about like a toddler.

Micara: Ah, what did I do, Mum?

Mrs Batou: I watched you dance like a practising streetwalker. Your waist was as swift as a butcher's machete. Why were you doing such a filthy thing?

Pata: Mum, things are not as you think. We're your daughters, and we know what is OK for us. We can't disgrace ourselves or this family.

Mrs Batou: Oh, look at you! Always intruding to answer questions meant for others. And you talk so confidently, sounding like a pious evangelist! Just simple rice and stew, you can't cook, can you, Pata?

Pata: I'll cook it with time, Mum. Don't bother yourself.

Mrs Batou: At what age?

Pata: Anytime soon.

Mrs Batou: Look at the size of your breasts! Your age mates have saggy breasts but they are independent. You're here flirting around with perky breasts. (*She sighs*)

Blackout

11

Scene 3

An uptown public garden. It is a chilly afternoon in midseason. There are fewer frequenters than usual. Mrs Batou and her friend, Mrs Bamen, are sitting in a less noisy section of the garden. Vendors walk across the lawns back and forth, advertising and selling pastries and other home items. The two friends sit close to each other on a chair-like concrete slab. Mrs Bamen is dressed in a casual office attire. Mrs Batou wears an embroidered, thin-strapped, cocktail dress.

Mrs Bamen: My sister, our friendship is highly blessed. We've stood strong in the midst of challenges.
,   We have cried together, we have rejoiced together. You have stood by me through thick and thin, and I have stood by you in good and bad weather. My dear friend, I desire nothing more than this spirit.

Mrs Batou: I'm all for you, my sister. If at any time you stand against me, I will be like a chick in the midst of sparrow hawks.

Mrs Bamen: I can't let you down, no matter what happens. Good friends are for better things. They're hard to find. Our children can't separate us. I know you're doing your best as a loving and devoted mother. But at   times, trials intrude to spoil our efforts.

	And that's why they say bad fate never announces its coming.
Mrs Batou:	You've said it all! Bad luck does not signal its arrival! It behaves like a carefree thief, who by himself decides where and when he should burgle.
Mrs Bamen:	Please, sit Micara down and talk to her. She's your elderly daughter. If you condone her actions, she'll send you to the grave without any warning signals. She can't be above you! You brought her into this world!
Mrs Batou:	I'm making efforts, Ma Bamen.
Mrs Bamen:	Triple your efforts! If you're not careful enough, this girl will break loose and go astray.
Mrs Batou:	Her sister is the lesser of two evils.
Mrs Bamen:	I talk about Micara because she frequents my home. I know very little about Pata. Dinga keeps coming home late at night, and her usual excuse is that she is with Micara. She recounts the same tale every day like a songbird.
Mrs Batou:	Hmmm, these girls are tricksters. Their mouths overflow with lies. To be candid, I have never let Dinga stay in my house above 8 p.m.
Mrs Bamen:	So, you see what 1 am saying? She sometimes comes back at 10 p.m.

Mrs Batou:	Aha, obviously from elsewhere, not from my house.
Mrs Bamen:	Micara has brought a strong negative influence on my daughter.
Mrs Batou:	(*A little dejected.*) I don't deny what you say! I know Dinga to be a good girl.
Mrs Bamen:	Since Dinga made friends with this Micara, all has not been well with my daughter's conduct. She has become too lazy to accomplish anything. She cooks food that only the pigs and he-goats can appreciate. Just observe the things she takes an interest in: dance, songs, films on TV channels and on You-Tube, Facebook chats, Skype, twitting, Snapchat, WhatsApp chats, birthday parties, weddings, beauty enhancers… Nothing about studies! She makes no efforts to learn cooking skills.
Mrs Batou:	I'm sorry about the negative influence of Micara on Dinga. But as we just resolved, they can't ruin our union.
Mrs Bamen:	Each time Dinga comes home, she claims she is from visiting Micara. If she does not mention Micara, she mentions other female friends like Felicia, Carina, Tecla, etc. Anyway, I don't care much about her crafty ways. The truth will come out some

	day. When her little belly will start swelling with a pregnancy, she'll point at a certain Cletus or Evans, not Felicia or Carina. And that's when I'll speak my mind and take a serious action.
Mrs Batou:	(*Laughing.*) Well, terrible! We don't wish them anything bad, though.
Mrs Bamen:	Not in the least! We're conscious of their little tricks. They take us for fools, but we're not fools! They won't push us to flex our arms and exchange blows. No, for God's sake!
Mrs Batou:	Ugh, they will regret their actions!
Mrs Bamen:	My daughter has become a stranger to me, and even to herself. I don't have her in the palm of my hand. She's lazy to a fault. In fact, she won't defeat a snail in a running contest. As a young woman, she isn't hygienic at all. She hates having a shower, and that's rather bad for a woman. Despite that, she's attracted to boys!
Mrs Batou:	Ha! That's exactly what I see in Micara and Pata. Girls must not disregard elementary rules of hygiene.
Mrs Bamen:	When I ask her to cook soup, she makes it too salty, and it ends up in the pigsty. Her phone is busier than bubbling water.

	It receives message alerts after every second.
Mrs Batou:	Those are experiences I live in my house. In our days, boys used to drop stones on housetops to signal their presence. Today, an alert tone on a girl's phone indicates a boy is waiting nearby. He can't call to her.
Mrs Bamen:	Yeah! If it's the case, she instantly paints her lips red. In fact, she will choose red for everything: shoes, dress, anklet, bra, cap, and so on.
Mrs Batou:	Then you see her sweating in cold weather. The next thing is she tells you she's going to study, as always, with a female classmate.
Mrs Bamen:	(*She waves her hands.*) Meanwhile she's going to listen to obscene talks from a rascally boy in a dark corner. You know better what the cunning boy will say and repeat a thousand times: "…You're so beautiful. I like your dress. You look wonderful. You enchant me like none other. I'll buy you jean trousers. I'll buy you a necklace. I'll buy you a diamond wristwatch on your birthday…" Can you imagine that! Maybe his mouth has tasted no food since sunrise. And he may stay famished till the next

sunrise. His wretched mum is on the farm, making ridges to sow yams, cassava and potatoes. Instead of helping her, he goes making vain promises to a partner in crime.

He'll keep crooning love tunes till nightfall. The girl will declare it's getting late; she wants to leave. Then he'll stand like a trunk, casting lustful looks at her, wishing the encounter just started. Listen to his last words: "Baby, sweetheart, take care, nice dreams, bye-byeeeee!"

Mrs Batou:	(*Laughing.*) Ha-ha! Ma Bamen, that's funny! You have a mastery of their cunning tactics. If I'm still alive, it's because I've mustered enough energy to stand their temptations.
Mrs Bamen:	Ma Batou, I want us to consider something. Let's ask Micara and Dinga to put an end to this unholy friendship.
Mrs Batou:	It's OK by me.
Mrs Bamen:	(*In a soft tone.*) This might not be best option, but I think it can fix one or two things. When we separate them, that'll bring an end to their complicity. When they no longer see each other, there'll be no sharing of bad ideas. Their bad plans will never

17

get out. So, that's my idea.

Mrs Batou:	It's a bright idea. We can't sit and watch them wander into destruction. At one moment, I made efforts to have Micara move and live with my sister, Pacha.
Mrs Bamen:	I quite remember, you told me about it. What happened you didn't proceed with the idea?
Mrs Batou:	I later thought better of it. I wanted her to go and be where she could breathe new air, get new companions, get new influences and anything that could reform her. But on second thoughts, I felt Micara might go and inflict pain on my sister. I am much less persevering than Pacha. She is a high blood patient. Can you imagine I'll send Micara to live with her?
Mrs Bamen:	Oh, you were right! With her high blood disease, she can't endure the caprices of a wayward adolescent girl like Micara.
Mrs Batou:	If I went ahead to execute my plan, it would mean I don't like my sister. Micara would send her to the grave in the twinkle of an eye.
Mrs Bamen:	Correct, you took a good decision. Actually, I guess your home has real

	problems. We all have problems, but your own problems bear horns and thorns.
Mrs Batou:	True, and I think there is a curse in my house. A few days ago, I told my husband that I suspect a curse from his family, and he got so offended.
Mrs Mamen:	Of course, he was right. What good evidence did you have for pointing a finger at his family?
Mrs Batou:	My maternal granny told me that some of his grandparents were evil people.
Mrs Bamen:	How true is that? Take your time and seek the truth. Seek the truth to your problems with frankness. No one, lowborn or highborn, will obscure the truth.

Blackout

ACT TWO
Scene 1

The Batous' sitting room at sunset. Micara sits at the dining table, scanning through a notebook. Mrs Batou approaches and sits on a sofa.

Mrs Batou:	(*In low tone.*) Come and let's talk.
Micara:	OK. (*She moves forward and sits on her own sofa.*)
Mrs Batou:	A serious decision has been taken against you.
Micara:	(*Disturbed.*) Hmmm! What is the decision about, Mum?
Mrs Batou:	Mrs Bamen has stamped out your friendship with Dinga. Henceforth, your presence in their house is undesirable. If you set foot there, they will kick you out. They will hire bouncers with beefy arms to harass and assault you!
Micara:	Did she seek your opinion before taking the decision?
Mrs Batou:	Yes, she spoke with me, and I felt it was most pertinent. You can only reap what you sow, my daughter.
Micara:	My Goodness, Mrs Bamen isn't a serious lady! She is just a mighty hypocrite.

Mrs Batou:	Please, just respect the decision by staying away from her daughter. Don't tempt Mrs Bamen! She works with the court, and she is highly connected.
Micara:	Ha, why did she take such a mad decision?
Mrs Batou:	Giving you details now is needless. However, let me summarise her concerns in a few words. She said you're a bad influence on Dinga. Of course, I've been telling you that. She said your friendship with Dinga has made Dinga wayward, coquettish, crafty and dirty.
Micara:	(*In anger.*) Ah, did you defend me when she uttered such bad things?
Mrs Batou:	How could I? You're guilty in one way or the other.
Micara:	I'm not guilty, Mum! You have to defend your children when they're insulted. You let your friend expose your child at her convenience; that's not fair. I'm your child; I deserve your protection! The Dinga you admire isn't an angel as you believe. She does horrible things behind her mum's back.
Mrs Batou:	Ah, she's your friend! Dirty pigs bathe together in the same mud.
Micara:	Mum, I'm big enough to imitate Dinga. Mrs Bamen knows very little

	about her. Dinga is a double-headed snake! In fact, I won't say anything more. But her mum should stop insulting me! One more insult against me, I'll expose her adulterous affairs with lawyers, magistrates and her co-workers. I know a lot about her infidelities. In fact, I hate pretenders!
Mrs Batou:	(*With bulging eyes.*) Shh! Watch your tongue! I think you know who Mrs Bamen is! Be ready to defend yourself when she charges you with slander. I will not be part of any litigation you instigate. You'll carry your own cross by yourself. That said I declare this topic closed!
Micara:	It's all right, Mum.
Mrs Batou:	Let's focus on what concerns us. Your conduct aside, your school results aren't good, to say the least. And there's only one reason for that - distraction. When you make yourself a carcass, you give out a bad smell.
Micara:	I'm taking the certificate exam next year, and I promise to make it.
Mrs Batou:	You are getting old. And you know it's a burden to keep grown-up girls at home for so long. I'm not saying you should engage and get married now. Further your studies and become a worthy lady; that's the dream of every mother.

Micara:	After obtaining my certificate, I'll do a professional training.
Mrs Batou:	That's a bright idea! But, because of the burdens you create here, your dad wants you married in the shortest possible time.
Micara:	Why is he in a hurry? Have I become excrement that must be disposed of?
Mrs Batou:	He's hastening your marriage for a reason. He isn't comfortable with what he sees and hears about you. And I share his concern.
Micara:	Oh, what does he see and hear about me?
Mrs Batou:	OK, just one example will suffice! There's one young boy that hangs around with you. He has the guts to walk in and out of this house at his leisure. I'm not by this saying you shouldn't have a friend! You are mature enough to direct your own steps. The young man is from a bad family. He's a blood relative of evil people. Not long ago, your father aimed his AK-47 rifle at his skull, and I held him back. The worst could have happened.

Micara:	I guess you are talking about Sala.
Mrs Batou:	That's the name. A raw fellow with bad manners!
Micara:	What's wrong with him, Mum? You have an extreme hatred for him, I see...
Mrs Batou:	A bellicose panther deserves a bullet on the forehead.
Micara:	He is my former schoolmate. I have nothing to do with him.
Mrs Batou:	(*Laughing.*) I was once a girl with bouncing breasts like yours. I was curvy and the talk of the town for a long time. The species of yams you eat today was eaten centuries ago. Not climbing on trees now doesn't mean I've never climbed on trees before.
Micara:	What's the problem with Sala, Mum?
Mrs Batou:	OK, incline your ears and listen. Sala's father was an expert thief. He exercised his job for over twenty years, and they say he murdered six people and wounded over a hundred others.
Micara:	Ugh! I can't believe what you are saying! (*She covers her mouth with her hands.*)
Mrs Batou:	I haven't finished my story yet! Sala's father stole over ninety cattle from cattlemen. He mistreated his enemies, maiming some of them. He burned his neighbour's house and stole foodstuffs from both well-to-do and miserable farmers. Sala's grandfather was called Sergeant Fanka.

Sergeant Fanka was a brave soldier who fought alongside the Germans during the First World War. When he returned from the war, he began committing crimes in the vicinity of his home. He pulled out a lady from matrimony and organised a hurried wedding with her. When the lady's husband raised his voice at him, Fanka got angry, tossed his firearm in the air, and the man took to his heels. He seized people's lands and no one pointed a finger at him.

Before his death, dozens of people perished in his cruel actions. His family was full of lepers, madmen, epileptic patients and cripples. I can recount more and more about them, but it's pointless. It's rather unfortunate, but there you go! We call that a malevolent family. They carry human blood on their hands. It's a no-go place for marriage! And as we say, a lion cannot bring forth a zebra.

Micara:	Mum, you seem to think he will suffer because of the crimes of his parents and grandparents.
Mrs. Batou:	Yeah, he is already suffering very badly.
Micara:	Why should he suffer?
Mrs Batou:	Ask the gods. When you sow, you reap and your descendants take turns in reaping as well.

Micara:	It isn't fair, Mum! I pay for the crimes of my parents, can you imagine that? But as I said, Mum, I have nothing to do with him.
Mrs Batou:	If Sala means it, you'll be his! How did the leper succeed in taking to wife the city belle? He crept towards her and offered nice gifts. At the beginning, he faced hurdles. The belle repeatedly turned down his request, but he carried on with his efforts. He persevered and gave more gifts, showed her his gracious and easy-going nature. He often spoke to her in a soft voice, and made sure he used polite speech. Despite his handicap, he was elegant, clean and tidy. He cheered her up with smiles, melodious names, and tons of praises. She liked his ways. He gave her dresses, jewels, shoes, and headscarves. And at last, to everyone's surprise, the belle fell for him, vowed to marry none other. They got the consent of their parents, and were happily united. Can you imagine that?
Micara:	Mum, I have nothing to do with Sala! What you've said about his family is heartbreaking. I didn't know he's from a bad family.
Mrs Batou:	(*With emphasis.*) I hope you've picked up something from my story.
Micara:	I have, of course, but I'm Micara, and not

	the belle in your story.
Mrs Batou:	The tactics the leper used can flatter the most vigilant girl.
Micara:	(*Shaking her head.*) Ha, not me!
Mrs Batou:	I'm just a patient observer! (*Micara goes far-off and calls Dinga on the phone.*)
Dinga:	(*She answers.*) Hello?
Micara:	You seem to be in a crowded area.
Dinga:	Yeah, let me withdraw from the area.
Micara:	Is it OK?
Dinga:	Yes!
Micara:	My mum told me something frustrating!
Dinga:	I'm aware of it. I was about to call you.
Micara:	They have put a stop to our friendship.
Dinga:	Yes, my mum was categorical about it.
Micara:	What's your opinion about the decision?
Dinga:	We have to respect it. But we can keep in touch through calls and texting.
Micara:	OK! My mum is also accusing me of dating Sala.
Dinga:	Oh, that is unfortunate! But is it true?
Micara:	No! He displays money around, but I can't submit to his trials.
Dinga:	So am I. My mum equally warned me against getting closer to him.
Micara:	I learnt he's from a bad family.
Dinga:	So they say. Hmmm, let's avoid him!
Micara:	OK, my dear, keep in touch, take care!
Dinga:	Thanks, bye! (*She hangs up.*)

The lights fade

Scene 2

Lights come on and brighten Mrs Batou's sitting room. There is half calm in the house. Soon, a low-pitch, amorous song begins playing in the background. Pesou stands adjacent the dining table, reading messages on his phone. There's an incoming call. He answers, "hello." The caller wishes him a happy birthday and hangs up. Petou's face glistens with joy. He gets on reading other messages.

Pesou:	Wow, I've received more than 1K birthday wishes.
Micara:	I'm happy for you.
Pata:	1K birthday wishes! You've become a pop star overnight, eh!
Pesou:	Yeah, I'm a superstar!
Micara:	Do I need to send you a birthday message?
Pesou:	What for? (*He continues reading new messages.*)
Pata:	(*She comes and stands by him and intones a song.*) Happy birthday to you, Happy birthday to you, Happy birthday to you, Pesou… Happy birthday to youuuu…! (*Micara claps with frenzy.*)
Micara:	Pata, your voice is cracked!
Pata:	That's true. I'll drink water to fix it.
Pesou:	And coffee, too.
Pata:	You're a clown, Pesou.

Micara:	Let's unveil the birthday cake. Pesou, keep away that phone and get ready! (*Pata gets a kitchen knife and gives to Pesou. He stoops and cuts the cake at its edge. Micara and Pata excite him with noisy claps. Micara gets the knife and slices the remaining cake into many pieces. They share it, fill their glasses and raised them in a toast to Pesou. Pata goes to the CD player and plays an exciting rap song. Pesou rises, holds Micara and they dance with slow steps. Pata joins them, and they all make merry in earnest. In a couple of minutes, beads of sweat start dropping down their faces. They are weary of dancing.*)
Pata:	You invited no one for your birthday.
Pesou:	Yeah, and you know why, don't you?
Pata:	I do. Ha! It's terrible with our parents!
Micara:	Mum said Sala should never set foot in this house. Dad almost killed him with his rifle.
Pesou:	Hey! Dad has to be careful! He has no license to own that weapon. A military drunkard abandoned it in a bar, and dad collected it and is claiming its ownership.
Micara:	That's a bad story, indeed!
Pata:	Mum says Dinga too should never set foot here.
Micara:	Ha, that's the worst!
Pesou:	Dad and mum may soon be back. Let's

	hurry up and keep away the glasses. Mum won't like to see us taking wine.
Pata:	You are right. That'll be another cause for endless scolding.
Micara:	She must understand this is a birthday party.
Pesou:	Maybe they didn't celebrate birthdays in their youthful days.
Micara:	Must they then stop us from celebrating because they didn't do so?
Pesou:	I think they want us to go through what they experienced.
Pata:	I'm not sure! Our maternal granny told me our mum was stubborn in her early life. I also learnt she loved fun very much.
Pesou:	Aha, and why is she against those who take an interest in fun?
Micara:	I think as parents, they want us to avoid the mistakes they made in their youth.
Pata:	I think so, but they are exaggerating. (*They hear approaching footsteps and adjust their postures. Mrs Batou and Mr Batou enter. Mrs Batou glances at her children. They wish Pesou a happy birthday. He responds with a gleeful face. Mrs Batou rises and makes towards the living room.*)
Mr Batou:	I can read joy on your faces. I hope you all enjoyed yourselves pretty well. (*They answer in unison. He looks high-spirited*

	and robust.)
Pesou:	Dad, would you like to drink something?
Mr Batou:	Yeah, what's available? *(He casts his eyes at the table.)*
Micara: you	We have red and white wine. Which do prefer?
Mr Batou:	Hmmm, a glass of red wine is good for me. (Pata *serves him a glassful of wine and two slices of cake.*)
Pata:	Enjoy yourself, Dad.
Mr Batou:	Cheers! *(He raises his glass. Pesou alone responds to the toast. The girls are no more drinking.)*
Micara:	We'll like to see Dad dance now.
MrBatou:	Really? OK, I'll do so, but with a dancing partner.
Pata:	Perfect! Your wife is in the room. Her attention is needed now!
Mr Batou:	Hold on a bit. When dancing time comes, we'll call her. Let me enjoy myself first. Wow, this wine has good taste! The cake too is well done. Bravo to the hand that baked it!
Pesou:	Thanks for appreciating, Dad. Would you like to have more wine?
Mr Batou:	Yeah, just one more glass, please. I've swilled so much beer in the gathering.
Micara:	Pesou, you'll soon get drunk! You have drunk well over two bottles of wine!
Mr Batou:	It's his birthday. But, he should drink with caution. Wine is deceptively sweet.

	It can turn your brain inside out.
Pesou:	That's true. But I'm drinking with a lot of caution.
Pata:	Can I call for Mum now?
Mr Batou:	Yes, I'm ready.
Micara:	Ha-ha! We'll see your latest dancing skills. (*Pata goes to call for Mrs Batou. In a few minutes, she returns, wearing a twisted face.*)
Pata:	Mum says she won't be part of any crazy dancing.
Mr Batou:	Crazy dancing! No problem; I'll do the crazy dancing by myself. A crazy dancer is a crazy man, I believe. And she's married to a crazy man, ha-ha...!
Pesou:	Micara, choose a good number for Dad.
Micara:	Dad, make your choice. I know you like ancient rhumba.
Mr Batou:	Oh, you know it! Any piece from Franco Luambo will awaken my spirits.
Pata:	Ha, that's ancient music from the late Congolese artiste.
Mr Batou:	Yes, he's dead, but his music is alive and valuable more than ever before. (*Micara plays Mario by Franco Luambo. Mr Batou springs to his feet and begins dancing. His legs and movements align with the speed and rhythm of the song. His children applaud as he changes styles. He is swifter and more flexible than most youths. Mrs Batou emerges,*

	tiptoes, and stands by her door, peeping through the edge of the door drape. Agitated, she darts into the sitting room.)
Mrs Batou:	Didn't I say it? The pleasure-seeking manners in these children come from you. Oh, look at what you promote in them…eating, dancing and drinking! And that's what you want them to embrace in their lives! It's regrettable, indeed!
Mr Batou:	Madam, take the floor! Let your children clap for your styles. They've applauded mine. Let's evaluate your own skills. Stop your shameful games! This is a birthday party. We do only one thing here: enjoy ourselves, ha-ha… *(He steps forward and enhances his dancing skills. Mrs Batou sees his moves as deliberate provocation.)*
Mrs Batou:	I'm wordless. I'll talk to you when you are sober. You're drunk. Look at the cake they baked! It has too much sugar!
Mr Batou:	I ate my own share, and found no excess sugar in it. I don't know what you're talking about. Let me have that piece for my stomach. Give it to me, please! *(She turns and dashes off in anger. Music continues playing, but there's no dancer to it. As the lights fade gradually, Mr Batou is seen staggering to the living room.)*

Scene 3

The visitor's sitting area in Mbola's courtyard. The noonday sun is a bit down. The set should portray a background with artefacts...carved chairs, woven mats, animal horns, statuettes, etc. Mr Mbola reclines on a wooden chair, casts an adoring gaze upon the surrounding verdure and the sky above. He's dressed in a woven jumper and a pair of gabardine trousers. On his head is a close-fitting kufi hat, knit with silk yarn. Mrs Batou appears, casually dressed in a kaftan.

Mrs Batou:	Greetings to you, my husband.
Mr Mbola:	*Bienvenue, ma chère épouse.* How is your husband and the children?
Mrs Batou:	(*She sighs.*) Ah, the usual problems have reached the apex.
Mr Mbola	But I believe everyone is in good health.
Mrs Batou:	Good health, yes! But when the body is strong and the mind unstable, we can only talk of a half-won victory.
Mr Mbola;	Oh, yeah! Now, what's at stake?
Mr Batou:	The stupidity of your brother and his children! They'll split my heart into pieces. Please, sit your brother down and talk to him. He has gone astray and is wandering into darkness. He has willfully aligned with the foolishness of his children. They have all become crazy dancers, big gluttons and rowdy drinkers; can you imagine that?
Mr Mbola:	If they dance, eat and drink with

Welcome, my dear wife.

34

moderation, then I find no fault with that. In this world, both the lowborn and the highborn indulge in enjoyment at various degrees.

Mrs Batou: My husband, they know nothing called moderation. They all fancy excesses. Their latest provocation was during Petou's birthday party at home. Your brother came to the party already in stupour. He ate to excess, he danced to excess, drank to excess, to the pleasure of his children. They all became his spectators, and they all mocked me, calling me a cheerless, old-fashioned woman. I stood there alone, with no one to see the least logic in my position as a mother. My husband, I'm a woman; I know about the pains of childbirth. No one should mock me!

Mr Mbola: Ma'am, what they did was wrong. He mustn't drink to stupour with his own children. He should cease vegetating with them! He's setting wrong examples. Your husband is a well-paid state agent. But he has a problem: he directs all his money towards pleasure ventures. Worst of all, he pampers his children, gives them too much liberty, lavishes gifts on them. How can he drink to drunkenness with his own children? It's unbelievable!

Mrs Batou: (*Throws her hands sideward.*) Imagine

how bad your night would be sleeping beside a drunken man! He would snore like an elephant, smell like rotten weed or some enormous carcass. His belly would rumble, and later, you would get noisy and smelly farts from his asshole. That's really what I go through in your brother's house, at least twice a week. Is that different from residing in hell, my husband?

Mr Mbola: Heh, too bad indeed, Ma'am! I'll talk to him. The lion does not bring forth a wolf. You reap what you sow.

Mrs Batou: (*Excited.*) Yeah! You've struck the point. It's never late to seek the truth. Ha, my marriage was done in haste! My parents didn't investigate your family, and that was wrong. I don't know much about your family history. It's wisdom for a family to know the past records of their would-be in-laws.

Mr Mbola: You're not wrong in your thinking. I'll tell you the truth. Maybe from there, you'll understand your husband better. You'll also know more about your children. Before I proceed, bear in mind that there's no perfect family anywhere under the sun. Families are like tribes and nations. They all share good and bad histories, and that's how the world was created.

Mrs Batou: I understand.

Mr Mbola:	My maternal grandma was a famous dancer.
Mrs Batou:	Ha! No doubt, I now see why my children are into crazy dancing.
Mr Mbola:	In her days, the movement of women was tightly controlled. For that reason, her dancing ended only in little enclosures. She, however, handed down her talent to her daughter (my own mum). And my mum went wild with her own dancing skills. She often attended feasts and came home at cockcrow. My dad was into excess drinking, his wife into excess dancing. The duo got tangled in these habits for decades.
Mrs Batou:	My goodness! I now know the cause of my problems.
Mr Mbola:	You don't call those problems, Ma'am! Between drinking and murdering, which do you prefer?
Mrs Batou:	Drinking.
Mr Mbola:	So, you have no problems as you claim. To be subtle, your problems are easy to handle. Your children are not thieves. Your husband is not a burglar. They're fun-loving people, and you can't hang them because of that.
Mrs Batou:	(*With mixed feelings.*) Thank you very much. You've given me a good of piece information. I will make good use of it.

37

| Mr Mbola: | (*He soliloquises.*) Every family has good and evil people. I'm not so reckless and senseless to name the real sinners of my family. I'm not so idiotic to reveal the darkest side of my ancestors. I can't be so foolish to unveil the secrets of our own monsters. Each family has its own monsters. And every family has its own saints. While discussing with her, I didn't mention the evil descendants of my family. My brother's wife is crafty, but I still have some sense in my head. I will always outsmart her crafty ways. (*He grins and walks offstage. The lights fade suddenly.*) |

ACT THREE
Scene 1

At sundown. Mrs Batou and her husband are relaxing on the veranda. The house is quiet as none of their children is at home. Bird chirps are resonating in the clearing before them.

Mrs Batou:	Really, I regret my past decisions. I was naïve and lacking in foresight. The outcome is horrible, and I now stand in tears like a tamed monkey.
Mr Batou:	What again, my dear? You look tense and unwell.
Mrs Batou:	When you love eating hard bones, your teeth will pay a price for that someday.
Mr Batou:	Please, make your words clear. I can't make out what you are saying.
Mrs Batou:	Ha, am I talking to a baby?
Mr Batou:	Come clean, I'm interested in what you want to say.
Mrs Batou:	My dear husband, the verdict has been passed! You're the cause of the darkness enclosing us in this home. I said this before, and you denied the fact.
Mr Batou:	(*Irritated.*) Oh, stop the jokes! What verdict and what darkness?
Mrs Batou:	Listen and listen well. Our children are a direct picture of you, your mum, your dad, and your grandparents.
Mr Batou:	What do you know about my family? Who whispered such shameless lies into your

39

	ears?
Mrs Batou:	Thank God, I sought the truth in earnest, and at last, I got it!
Mr Batou:	Who enlightened you about my family?
Mrs Batou:	Your elder brother is the holder of the truth. I got the truth from the horse's mouth. You can't dispute anything about it. You've been defending yourself, claiming to be an angel, but oh, the truth is out.
Mr Batou:	My brother is making a mockery of himself. I didn't know he could be so stupid. How can an ageing man gossip like a she-goat?
Mrs Batou:	Get the facts clear, my husband! The truth does not kill anyone. It heals festering wounds. Get the facts clear in your head. Your mum was an excessive dancer; you can't deny it. Your dad too was an excessive drinker; you can't deny it. And lastly, your grandparents indulged in all kinds of excesses. I have not added nor have I subtracted a word from the facts. I just relayed them as I got them. Look at where I directed my destiny! Poor me!
Mr Batou:	My dear wife, I've keenly listened to your vexation. At this age, you should know how to filter the words that come to your ears. You don't commit empty words into your memory. My brother is universally known for running his mouth like a thieving whore. Perhaps he's jealous of me, who cares? Perhaps he wants me dead so that he can take charge of you, who knows?

	Perhaps he has lost his mind because of the pangs of poor living, who knows? Perhaps, because of too much frustration, he delights in talking for the sake of it, who knows? Nevertheless, whatsoever prompted him to broadcast this childish information, let me remind you that, without exception,
	gluttons, drunkards and dancers are found in all families.
Mrs Batou:	(*Objecting.*) That's not true! Prove your point by naming any of such persons in my family.
Mr Batou:	Playing the blame game won't help us now. In a situation like this one, you should calm down your mind. Think of possible headways. You can elect to atone the gods; they too have a role to play. On your own, you can use high tactics to raise your children in a proper way. You can seek the help of moral instructors, youth counsellors and animators, and authentic men of God. Be tolerant enough to seek solutions where you most need them.
Mrs Batou:	How do you raise children imbued with family blood habits?
Mr Batou:	A thief today, a pastor tomorrow! Haven't you come across that? Get to work, and reform your children to become responsible adults.
Mrs Batou:	Hmmm, you want me to drain the blood in them and transfuse new blood, don't you? You talk much about them, what about you? Your own conduct needs overhaul as well.

41

	And how can anyone aspire to repair the conduct of an aged man? Can you deny an old monkey from climbing trees?
Mr Batou:	You're insulting me, and that shows your lack of manners. You can't correct a wrong by infusing it with multiple curses. I didn't drop from the heavens. I came out of a woman's womb, and I advise you to respect that woman. Also respect the man that hooked up with her to bring me forth. If you don't respect them, let's go to the law court and annul the marriage.
Mrs Batou:	Heh, why are you saying such odd things?
Mr Batou:	You're insulting my parents and my grandparents! You treat them with despise and disgust. That's what no woman should do. Learn to understand the destiny that tied us together. (*Mrs Batou stays quiet, rolling her eyes side by side. They soon walk to the living room.*)

Scene 2

It's 10 a.m. Micara and Pata are busy with laundry at the courtyard. Pesou is ironing clothes at the doorway. Mrs Batou and her husband are sitting in the middle of the courtyard, relaxing and enjoying the cold morning air. Of a sudden, two policemen emerge at the entrance to their home. They're walking briskly, wearing unfriendly faces.

Mrs Batou: (*Glances at them and whispers to her husband.*) What the hell do they want? I hate the sight of these people.

Mr Batou: Hold your patience! We'll soon know their mission.

Mrs Batou: I hope they're not bringing bad news.

Inspector Wokem: Greetings to everyone here. I'm Inspector Daniel Wokem of the Sixth Police District Post. Meet Constable Derick Pokem; we work at the same post. We're in search of a certain Elvis Pesou, a student of Trinity High School. Does anyone know him, please?

Mrs Batou: (*Silent and ponderous.*) Elvis Pesou, you mean?

Constable Pokem: Yes, Madam! (He *opens a file and reads the name audibly for confirmation.*)

Pesou: (*He mutters in a quavering voice.*) Here I am. (*Micara and Pata abandon their chores and join the scene. They look confused,*

	open-mouthed.)
Inspector Wokem:	(*In an intimidating tone.*) Present your ID card!
Pesou:	I have the school ID card.
Constable Pokem:	No problem, present it. Let's be sure you're the person wanted. (*Pesou goes into the room and gets his school ID card.*)
Mr Batou:	What's the matter, Officers?
Inspector Wokem:	Just hold on for a while.
Mrs Batou:	What crime has my son committed?
Constable Pokem:	Be patient, you'll soon know. (*They observe the school ID card with keen interest.*)
Inspector Wokem:	Suspect identity confirmed! OK, this is the individual we're looking for. (*He removes a search warrant from a file and holds it out.*) Do you have a room of your own?
Pesou:	Yes, Sir.
Inspector Wokem:	Let's get there! (*They make towards Pesou's room.*)
Micara:	(*With hands on her head.*) Oh, we're dead!
Pata:	I had a bad dream last night, but didn't know it was an ill omen.
Inspector Wokem:	(*to his colleague.*) Make sure you search under the bed.
Constable Pokem:	Ah, I have got it! (*he holds up a flat, king-size Casio piano.*)
Inspector Wokem:	(*Smiling.*) Bravo! It's a brand new piano! (*They walk out of the room,*

44

	holding Pesou.)
Micara:	Hmmm, he's under arrest! That's Sala's piano.
Pata:	Are you sure?
Micara:	Yeah.
Inspector Wokem:	(*Turns to Mr and Mrs Batou.*) Don't get worried. Your son is still a suspect. He's caught with a stolen piano.
Mrs Batou:	Jesus! A stolen piano!
Constable Pokem:	Have a look at it, Madam!
Inspector Wokem:	Pesou, read this document carefully and sign it. (*He reads in haste and signs it.*) As I said earlier, there's no cause for worry. This is his arrest warrant. We'll take him to our post for questioning. This piano is a stolen good. He's charged as a receiver of a stolen good. He has to prove himself innocent or not, as the case goes on. It's not a serious criminal offence; that's why he's not in handcuffs. (*They take Pesou along.*)
Mrs Batou:	What have I done to merit this? (*Mr Batou quickly dresses up and follows them.*)
Mr Batou:	I'll be back soon. (*The scene switches to a half-dark area offstage. The lights are faint and the speakers are less audible.*)
Inspector Wokem:	I like people who react promptly like you. If you don't work hard, your son will serve a five-year jail term.
Mr Batou:	Officer, I don't want that to happen. That's the only son I have.
Inspector Wokem:	Get the facts of the case before we discuss

Inspector Wokem: There's a notorious thief here called Sala, do you know him?

Mr Batou: Yes, I do.

Inspector Wokem: Oh, how could you allow such a fellow to befriend your son?

Mr Batou: He's not my son's friend! He comes to my house uninvited. I recently barred him from trespassing my compound.

Inspector Wokem: The piano is stolen by him. It belongs to the principal of Greenland City College. When he robbed the principal's house, someone saw him at the time of escape and informed us about the robbery. We searched and arrested him. Upon questioning him, he told us the piano was with your son. That's the story!

Mr Batou: Officer, I'm a state agent with a meagre salary. However, I'm ready to do something to guarantee the release of my son.

Inspector Wokem: His release can't be as easy as you think. A stolen good has been found in his keeping. That's too bad! The law must take its course!

Mr Batou: It might be a setup by Sala. He might have planned vengeance as I barred him from coming to my house.

Inspector Wokem: That's of little concern to us! You have to see me, see my colleague, see our boss (Senior Superintendent Akam), and the state council (Chief Justice Ako). That entails money, I must specify!

Mr Batou: Ha, it's no easy affair, Officer! How much

	can I offer?
Inspector Wokem:	I deserve one hundred thousand francs, my colleague will get eighty, my boss will be given two hundred, and the state council will receive three hundred.
Mr Batou:	Oh, so much money! Where will I get it from, Officer?
Inspector Wokem:	I kept it minimal because I know you don't have the means. It's the least we can take, just to help you. If you don't have it, your son will serve a jail term. So, you must respond quickly! Get back and begin raising the money. No bargain, please!
Mr Batou:	Thank you, Officer. (He *goes back to his house*.)
Mrs Batou:	(*Observing his facial looks*.) Have you bargained his release with the officers?
Mr Batou:	Yes, I have, but it's a bad bargain! So much money is required.
Mrs Batou:	How much are they asking for?
Mr Batou:	Six hundred and eighty thousand francs.
Mrs Batou:	Hmmm, so exorbitant! That amount is big enough to settle a bride price.
Mr Batou:	Very true. We are in deep shit!
Mrs Batou:	Don't bother; stop the negotiations with them for now. (*She dresses up and picks up her hand bag.*)
Mr Batou:	Where are you going now?
Mrs Batou:	I want to see my friend, Mrs Bamen.
Mr Batou:	Ah, a salient idea! She's a court clerk. She's well positioned to plead our cause.
Mrs Batou:	Yes, and this matter must pass through her

	hands.
Mr Batou:	Are you sure she'll exert much influence in our favour?
Mrs Batou:	Of course! She's very connected; she's a formidable woman.
Mr Batou:	Well, let's count on her. When you get soaked up, any fabric can dry your body.
Mrs Batou:	I must get going now.
Mr Batou:	All right, see you later. (*She darts away. Micara and Pata come towards their dad.*)
Micara:	Dad, where's he now?
Mr Batou:	He has been taken into custody.
Mr Batou:	Oh my God!
Pata:	That piano is the evil plan of Sala.
Mr Batou:	Didn't I tell you to avoid him? Look at the harm he has caused us! Just because we barred him from coming here!
Micara:	We can't conclude that he used the piano as a trap.
Mr Batou:	You want to support Sala, don't you? I've been monitoring your activities. He doesn't come here for Pesou. Pesou is just a bridge he crosses to see you. I've been observing that for long, my daughter.
Micara:	That's not true, Dad!
Mr Batou:	Shh! That's not even our concern for now. (*He turns and walks away.*)

The lights fade off on them.

48

SCENE 3

Mrs Batou meets Mrs Bamen at home. The former's face glistens with sweat provoked by brisk walking. She is panting like a famished wolf.

Mrs Batou:	My dear friend, there's fire on my head!
Mrs Bamen:	What has gone wrong?
Mrs Batou:	Pesou has been placed under police custody. He'll be questioned for keeping a stolen piano.
Mrs Bamen:	A stolen piano!
Mrs Batou:	Yes, my sister!
Mrs Bamen: he	What's he doing with a piano? Has become a musician?
Mrs Batou:	I can't answer that question, my sister. Their love for music is what will bring them doom. What you cherish to excess is what shall send you to the grave.
Mrs Bamen:	How did he get the piano?
Mrs Batou:	Sala stole it from a school principal.
Mrs Bamen:	Oh, that wayward boy again! I almost went insane when I saw him chatting with Dinga last week.
Mrs Batou:	Beware of that young man; he can harm your daughter.
Mrs Bamen:	I warned Dinga to avoid keeping company with him.
Mrs Batou:	I ordered him never to trespass my

49

	premises. Perhaps because of my decision, he has sought vengeance.
Mrs Bamen:	I learnt he goes around tempting girls with stolen money.
Mrs Batou:	My dear friend, our son is in custody, and the police are demanding six hundred and eighty thousand francs for his release. They say if the sum is paid, there'll be no further action against him.
Mrs Bamen:	The amount is too high!
Mrs Batou:	True! I'm barely managing a hand-to-mouth life with my husband. How do I raise such a sum?
Mrs Bamen:	Give me three hundred thousand francs, and consider the case a fait accompli.
Mrs Batou:	Thank you very much, my sister. That can't be above us.
Mrs Bamen:	When the case file reaches me, I'll make it disappear. I'll do so in complicity with Chief Justice Ako. He's my confidant. When the file is declared missing in court, the matter will be discharged for lack of evidence. Then the suspects will be acquitted.
Mrs Batou:	(*Smiling.*) In fact, I'll be pleased to see my son out of this mess.
Mrs Bamen:	Put your trust in me.
Mrs Batou:	Thanks in advance.
Mrs Bamen:	Make the money available to me within three days.
Mrs Batou:	We'll do so; it's no big deal.
Mrs Bamen:	I wish you the best in your efforts. (*Mrs Batou walks away.*)

SCENE 4

Mrs Batou sits alone, listening to a church hymn. Pata darts into the sitting room, visibly eager to talk.

Pata:	Mum, something unusual has happened.
Mr Batou:	Stop the music! *(She goes to the CD player and switches it off.)*
Pata:	Micara has packed her belongings and escaped.
Mrs Batou:	*(Rises to her feet.)* Is she already far away?
Pata:	Yes, she used a motorbike for fear of delays at the bus station.
Mrs Batou:	Oh, you're not serious! Weren't you aware of her plan to escape?
Pata:	I wasn't aware of anything. I saw her heading off to the town on a bike with her valise. Yesterday, she said she would visit Ma Pacha, but didn't mention when.
Mrs Batou:	Ma Pacha, my sister! A high blood patient! She must return without delay! Why is she escaping from the house, by the way?
Pata:	Mum, I don't want to break your heart. There's bad news in the air!
Mrs Batou:	I'm already familiar with bad news. Break the news to me without any fear.
Pata:	Micara is pregnant!
Mrs Batou:	Jesus! *(She sits backward. Pata grips her arms affectionately.)*
Pata:	Take it easy, Mum!
Mrs Batou:	Bring me water to drink. (*Water is brought*

Mrs Batou:	Who made her pregnant?
Pata:	Sala.
Mrs Batou:	Who? (*She drops and goes unconscious. Gripped by panic, Pata shouts at the top of her voice, calling for help. She fans air on her with a notebook. Mr Batou enters.*)
Mr Batou:	What's going on here?
Pata:	(*Panicking.*) Mum has passed out.
Mr Batou:	(*Bends and examines her heartbeat.*) Did she complain of any illness?
Pata:	No, Dad. She got some bad news.
Mr Batou:	What's the bad news about?
Pata:	Micara is pregnant! And she has escaped to Ma Pacha's house.
Mr Batou:	Go for a motorbike, let's rush her to the clinic. (*Pata runs out and soon returns with a biker. Mrs Batou is taken to a nearby clinic. As she's being attended to by the nurses, Mr Batou steps aside to converse with Pata.*)
Pata:	Dad, what about Pesou?
Mr Batou:	His situation is promising. I just transferred some money to Mrs Bamen. He'll be released anytime soon.
Pata:	(*Excited.*) I'll be happy!
Mr Batou:	Who made Micara pregnant?
Pata:	Sala.
Mr Batou:	Ah! I saw this coming. She won't terminate

	the pregnancy, anyway. But, it's a pity that she chooses to make and nurture a bastard.
Pata:	A bastard?
Mr Batou:	Yes, a bastard!
Pata:	Why that? Sala is alive...and a likely suitor.
Mr Batou:	I don't deny it. But do you consider that scarecrow a human being? Can he raise a normal child? Is he qualified to be my in-law? My daughter, let me be frank with you. That child shall be born a bastard! (*Mrs Batou regains her consciousness, but looks a little frail and unbalanced. She is carried back home on another motorbike.*)
Mrs Batou:	(*In a shaky voice.*) My husband, the world has gone crazy. Mrs Bamen just called informing me Dinga is pregnant.
Mr Batou:	Aha! Dinga and Micara pregnant at the same time!
Pata:	Hmmm, this matter is not easy!
Mrs Batou:	What matter? What difference will you make? (*Pata stays quiet.*)
Mr Batou:	Children have gone crazy!
Mrs Batou:	Sala is the author of Dinga's pregnancy.
Mr Batou:	Sala again! That yokel deserves a death penalty. I trust in Mrs Bamen. She'll use her connections to bring him down to nothing.
Mrs Batou:	That boy is out to destroy all of us. Ouch, I feel pains all over my body. Pata, bring me some water to drink. (*Water is brought in a mug and she drinks.*)

53

Mr Batou:	Didn't you tell me Dinga is well-behaved and wise?
Mrs Batou:	Please, leave me alone! I don't know what has gone wrong with her.
Mr Batou:	Sala is about twenty-two and Dinga ...oh just thirteen.
Mrs Batou:	Yeah, she's underage! She's below the age of consent, and for that reason, Mrs Bamen will have Sala jailed without any friction.
Mr Batou:	Micara is fourteen years old. She too is below the age of consent. But since we have no means to pursue Sala in court, we'll simply sit and benefit from Mrs Bamen's actions against him.
Mrs Batou:	My fear is that Dinga's pregnancy might distort the court procedure.
Mr Batou:	Well, Mrs Bamen knows what to do.

The scene blacks out

SCENE 5

Mrs Batou is fully recovered, but her spirit remains dampened with sad feelings.

Mrs Batou:	I've asked my sister to send Micara back to me.
Mr Batou:	That's normal. Micara shouldn't be a burden to Ma Pacha. And she's even a patient! We're her parents; let's bear the burden with her.
Mrs Batou:	I'm against abortion.
Mr Batou:	So am I.
Mrs Batou:	My friend too says Dinga won't abort the pregnancy.
Mr Batou:	Oh, it's a pity that our first grandchild is a bastard.
Mrs Batou:	Same thing with Mrs Bamen. We're not suffering the bad fate alone.
Mr Batou:	I pity her for not knowing who her daughter is.
Mrs Batou:	It's difficult to read the character of a girl. But I still maintain that Dinga is not a bad girl. It's just that Sala was too smart for them.
Mr Batou:	But they were sufficiently cautioned to avoid him.
Mrs Batou:	True, but he has powerful seductive tactics. He's able to mess up highly educated ladies. And I don't believe he uses potent charms.

Mr Batou:	Are we expecting the release of Pesou tomorrow?
Mrs Batou:	No, things have changed.
Mr Batou:	What has changed?
Mrs Bato:	Mrs Bamen says if she makes the case file disappear, Sala too will be set free. And you know best, Sala can't go free just like that!
Mr Batou:	Yeah, he has to be prosecuted for making an underage pregnant.
Mrs Batou:	Pesou's release is bound to delay because of that.
Mr Batou:	All we want is his liberty. If he gains it even after a week, no problem.
Mrs Batou:	Mrs Bamen says she'll do all in her power to ensure Sala gets a maximum jail term.
Mr Batou:	That's very possible. She has the necessary connections at her disposal. (*There's a sudden noise nearby. Inspector Wokem and Constable Pokem march into the scene with tense faces.*)
Mrs Batou:	(*In an aside.*) These men again? I loathe their sight!
Inspector Wokem:	(*Without greeting anyone, he opens a file and scans through a few pages.*) Mr Batou, present your ID card, quickly! (*Mr Batou presents his card and stands still, worried.*)
Constable Pokem:	This is your search warrant. (*He shows it to Mr Batou.*)

	It confers upon us the power to search this home. Co-operate with us, please.
Mrs Batou:	Is there another stolen item in this house? (*She is ignored by the policemen. The entire house is searched in anger and with words of intimidation. Mr Batou maintains his calm. The policemen search various rooms, the kitchen and the barn.*)
Constable Pokem:	Oh, I have seen it! (*He holds out an AK-47 rifle and raises a knowing smile.*)
Inspector Wokem:	* *Ce monsieur n'est pas sérieux!*
Mrs Batou:	(*To herself.*) Oh my God! Another mighty trouble! This is really a year of tragedy in this home.
Inspector Wokem:	Mr Batou, come forward! Do you have the licence to own this weapon?
Mr Batou:	(*In a humble tone.*) No, Officer.
Inspector Wokem:	You'll be charged with keeping a firearm without a licence.
Mr Batou:	A drunken man abandoned it in a bar, and I picked it up.
Inspector Wokem:	Good, you picked it up, and it became yours, didn't it?
Constable Pokem:	Are you a soldier?
Mr Batou:	No, Officer! I didn't know it could implicate me.
Inspector Wokem:	Chief Justice Ako is better placed to interrogate you. You're under arrest, Sir! Constable Pokem, take charge of him! (*Mr Batou is handcuffed.*)
Mr Batou:	Officers, let's work out something and end the matter here.

* *This man is not serious!*

Inspector Wokem:	Ha-ha! *_Il nous prend pour des imbéciles._
Constable Pokem:	He's a joker! When we reached an agreement last time, did you honour your engagement?
Mr Batou:	I'm very sorry, Officers!
Inspector Wokem:	We arranged that you should see me, see my co-worker and my bosses. Did you do that? Instead, you secretly worked out the release of your son with a promiscuous court clerk. Now you say you're ready to agree with us! Once bitten, twice shy!
Constable Pokem:	He'll agree with himself! You'll face the wrath of justice! It serves you right.
Inspector Wokem:	He thinks he's smarter than police officers!
Constable Pokem:	Sala has implicated you. He informed us you own a war rifle. You should blame yourself for what you are going through. (_They take him away. Mrs Batou and Pata are seen screaming and invoking the Supreme God. In a short while, Mrs Batou is seen auctioning her house to a well-off butcher._)
Mrs Batou:	(_She monologues in undertones._) I have no choice! I'm obliged to sell this house. My son and my husband must be free! Micara, too, will soon be here to give birth, and the doctors

*_He's taking us for fools._

58

will impose a caesarian delivery. I will have to buy layette items for Micara's child. All that requires money. Where do I get the money from, if I don't sell this house? *(Inspector Wokem resurfaces.)*

Inspector Wokem:	Have you succeeded, Madam?
Mrs Batou:	Yes, Officer. *(She hands him one million five hundred thousand francs. The policeman counts the money with keen attention, nodding in appreciation. He smiles and slides the notes into his wallet.)*
Inspector Wokem:	Good! Your son will be released tomorrow. Your husband will come out in forty-eight hours. Caution your husband to be wise next time. He should never dare police officers!
Mrs Batou:	I will do. Thank you, Officer! May God bless you!

(The policeman takes off, beaming with joy. Mrs Batou and Pata are seen packing their belongings to move to a flat they have rented.)

The End

Printed in the United States
by Baker & Taylor Publisher Services